THE RUN

by Barroux

ALADDIN

New York London Toronto Sydney New Delhi

To my sister, B

ALADDIN · An imprint of Simon & Schuster Children's Publishing Division · 1230 Avenue of the Americas, New York, New York 10020 · First Aladdin hardcover edition August 2020 · Copyright © 2020 by Barroux · All rights reserved, including the right of reproduction in whole or in part in any form. · ALADDIN and related logo are registered trademarks of Simon & Schuster, Inc. For information about special discounts for bulk purchases, please contact Simon & Schuster Special Sales at 1–866–506–1949 or business@simonandschuster.com. The Simon & Schuster Speakers Bureau can bring authors to your live event. For more information or to book an event contact the Simon & Schuster Speakers Bureau at 1–866–248–3049 or visit our website at www.simonspeakers.com. · Designed by Laura Lyn DiSiena · The illustrations for this book were rendered on paper with acrylic paint and colored pencils. · The text of this book was set in Noyh. · Manufactured in China 0520 SCP · 2 4 6 8 10 9 7 5 3 1 · Library of Congress Control Number 2019944280 · ISBN 978-1-5344-0886-9 (hc) · ISBN 978-1-5344-0887-6 (eBook)

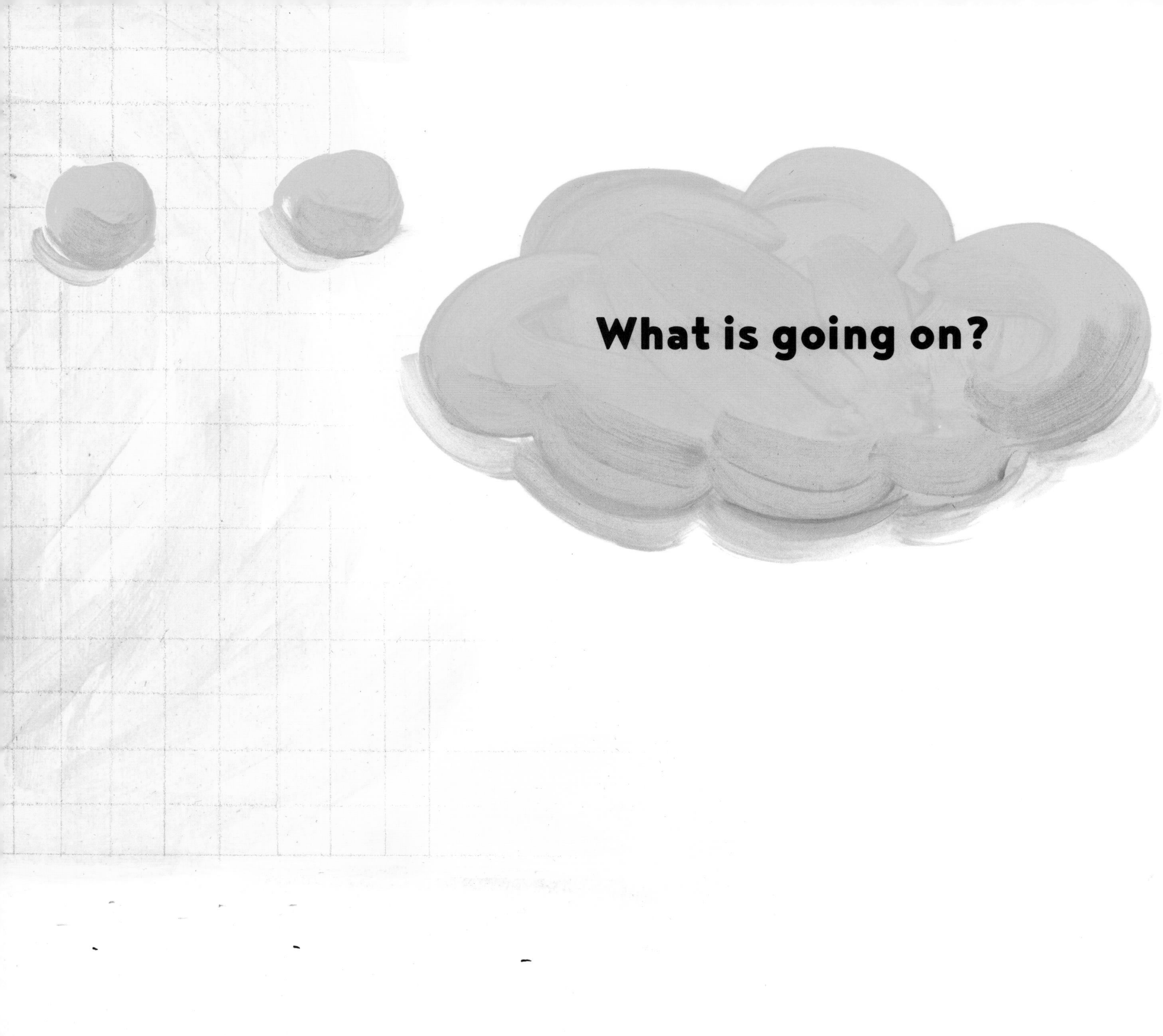
What is going on?

Gee, what a strange book.

Why are they all running?

It's a mystery!

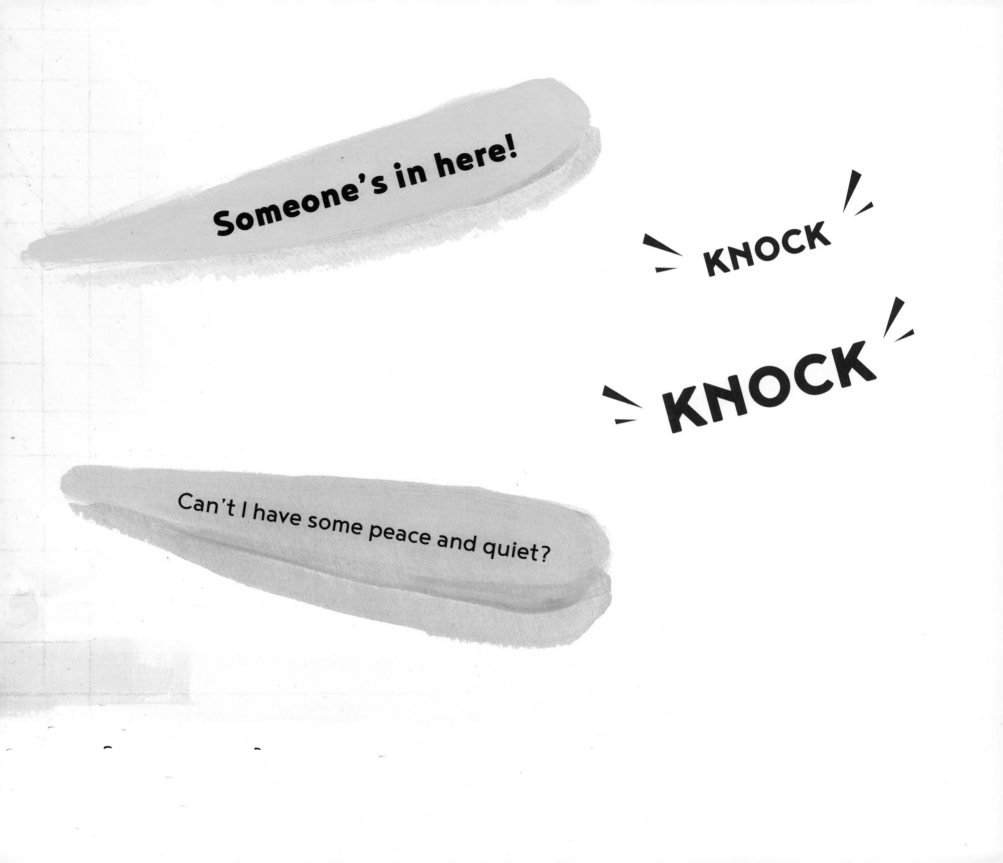